Fox-Davies, Dick
 Pilot's computer.–(Computers in action)
 1. Air pilots–Training of–Data processing
 –Juvenile literature 2. Aeronautics,
 Commercial–Juvenile literature–Data
 processing
 I. Title   II. Fiddy, Pamela   III. Series
 629.132′5216′02854   TL563
 ISBN 0–7136–2804–9

A & C Black (Publishers) Limited
35 Bedford Row, London WC1R 4JH

© 1986 Dick Fox-Davies and Pamela Fiddy

Acknowledgements
Illustrations by John Shackell
Photographs by: Chris Fairclough, pages 4, 5, 6, 7, 11, 12, 13, 14, 16, 18, 22 (top); Rediffusion Simulation Limited, Pages 10, 20, 21, 22 (bottom), 23, Cover, Britannia Airways Ltd, page 2.

The authors and publisher would like to thank Captain P. A. Mackenzie and the staff of British Caledonian Flight Training (formerly American Airlines Training Limited), Rediffusion Simulation Limited, Mr Amrit Row and Mr Stephen Robinson, without whose help and co-operation this book would not have been possible.

All rights reserved. No part of this publication may be reproduced, stored in a retrieval system, or transmitted in any form or by any means, electronic, mechanical, photocopying, recording or otherwise, without the prior permission in writing of A & C Black (Publishers) Limited.

Typeset by August Filmsetting, Haydock, St Helens
Printed in Singapore by Tien Wah Press (Pte) Limited

Pilot's Computer

Dick Fox-Davies and Pamela Fiddy

Contents

Introduction 2
The pilot's classroom 4
The simulator 10
The work of the computer 12
Sound and movement 14
What the pilot sees 16
Making the pictures 18
Flying in difficult conditions 20
The pilot's instructor 22
What else could simulators be used for? 24

A & C Black · London

Introduction

Have you ever needed help with a problem or a difficult job? Was it the kind of help a computer could give?

This book looks at how computers can help when people are learning to use expensive or dangerous new machines. It shows how computers can help pilots learn to fly different types of planes.

When you first learn to ride a bike, you can easily fall off. But if you go slowly, or start by riding on soft grass, nothing too bad will happen to you, or to the bike.

The first time that a pilot tries out a new type of plane, even if he's a very good and experienced pilot, there's a chance that he'll make one or two mistakes. If he made a bad mistake, it could be very dangerous. So every pilot needs to have extra training before flying a new type of plane.

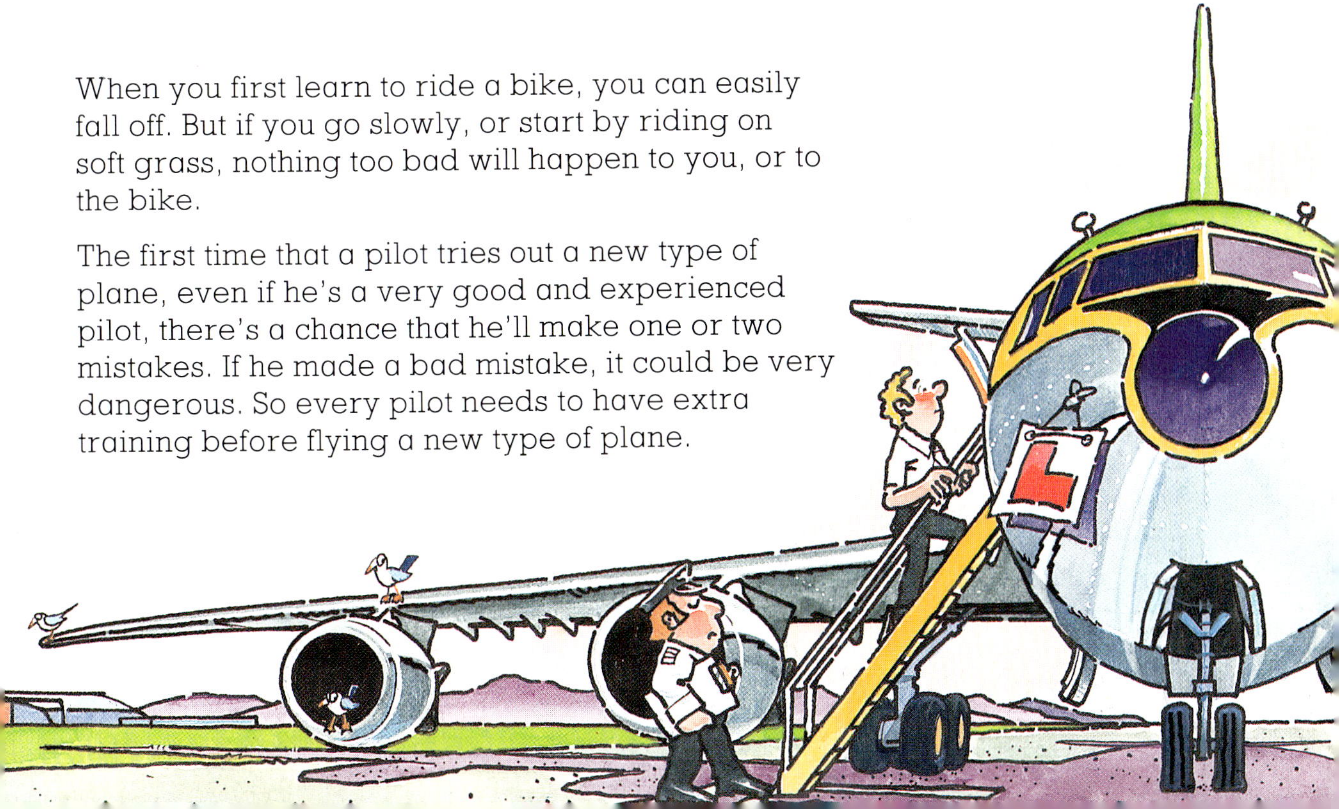

The pilot's classroom

In modern planes, there are hundreds of switches and levers and dials. When a pilot is learning to fly a new type of plane, he first has to learn where all the different switches are. He does this by practising in a model of the pilot's cabin.

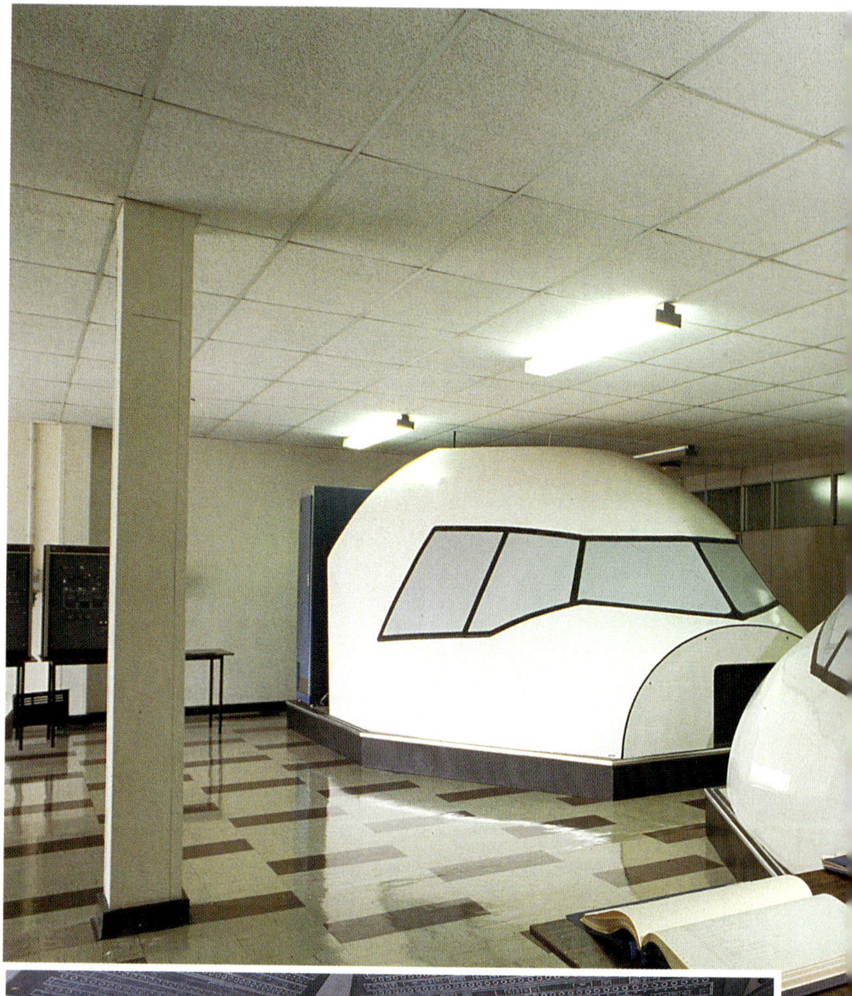

The model is the same size as the cabin of a real plane. It's fixed to the floor in a big room at the pilots' training school.

Inside the model, all the controls are laid out in the right places and there are seats for the pilot, the co-pilot and the engineer.

Some of the controls and switches move and work just like they would in a real plane. Some of them are just pretend; put there so that the pilot knows where he would find them in a real plane.

The chairs inside the model are quite ordinary. They're not the special seats that pilots and engineers have in real planes.

While the crew are just learning to find the controls, they don't need to have every single switch working and they don't need to sit in special chairs. This means that the models are not too expensive to make.

Each time a pilot takes a plane up into the air, he has to go through a special list of checks to make sure that everything is ready for take-off.

He has to check that the engines are running properly, the controls are working and he has enough fuel for the journey. When the plane lands, the pilot has to go through a different check-list.

The check-lists are quite long and it's very important that everything is remembered and checked in the right order.

Sitting in the model of the cabin, the pilot the co-pilot and the engineer can practise again and again until they are quite sure that they know what to do. Their instructor can sit with them and help them practise.

The crew also have lists of exactly what they should do if anything goes wrong with the plane while it is in the air.

If one of the engines caught fire, there wouldn't be time for the pilot to look in a book and find out what to do. So while they are sitting safely in the model, the pilot and his crew can practise what they would do if there was a serious emergency.

It doesn't matter if they make a few mistakes while they are learning. The model is safely on the ground so it can't crash and no-one can get hurt.

When you learn to ride a bike, you have to start by finding out how to use all the controls. You could do this by practising on a model. But if the model doesn't move, you won't know what it really feels like to ride on the road.

The pilot has the same problem. What he needs is something that is as safe as a model but feels just like a real plane.

Imagine how you could make a model like this.

First you would need a machine to lift the model off the ground and move it up and down as if it was flying.

Then you would have to do something about the view. Perhaps someone could hold pictures of the sky and the ground in front of the cabin window?

What about sound effects? Someone could stand behind the pilot making noises like an aeroplane's engines.

It wouldn't work, would it? The people moving the flying machine or holding up the pictures wouldn't know when to make the right effects. They wouldn't be able to see what the pilot was doing – or if he was moving the controls to go up or down. Even if they did know what to do, they wouldn't be able to change the pictures fast enough.

This is where someone had a good idea. They decided to use a computer to help the pilot feel as if he was in a real plane.

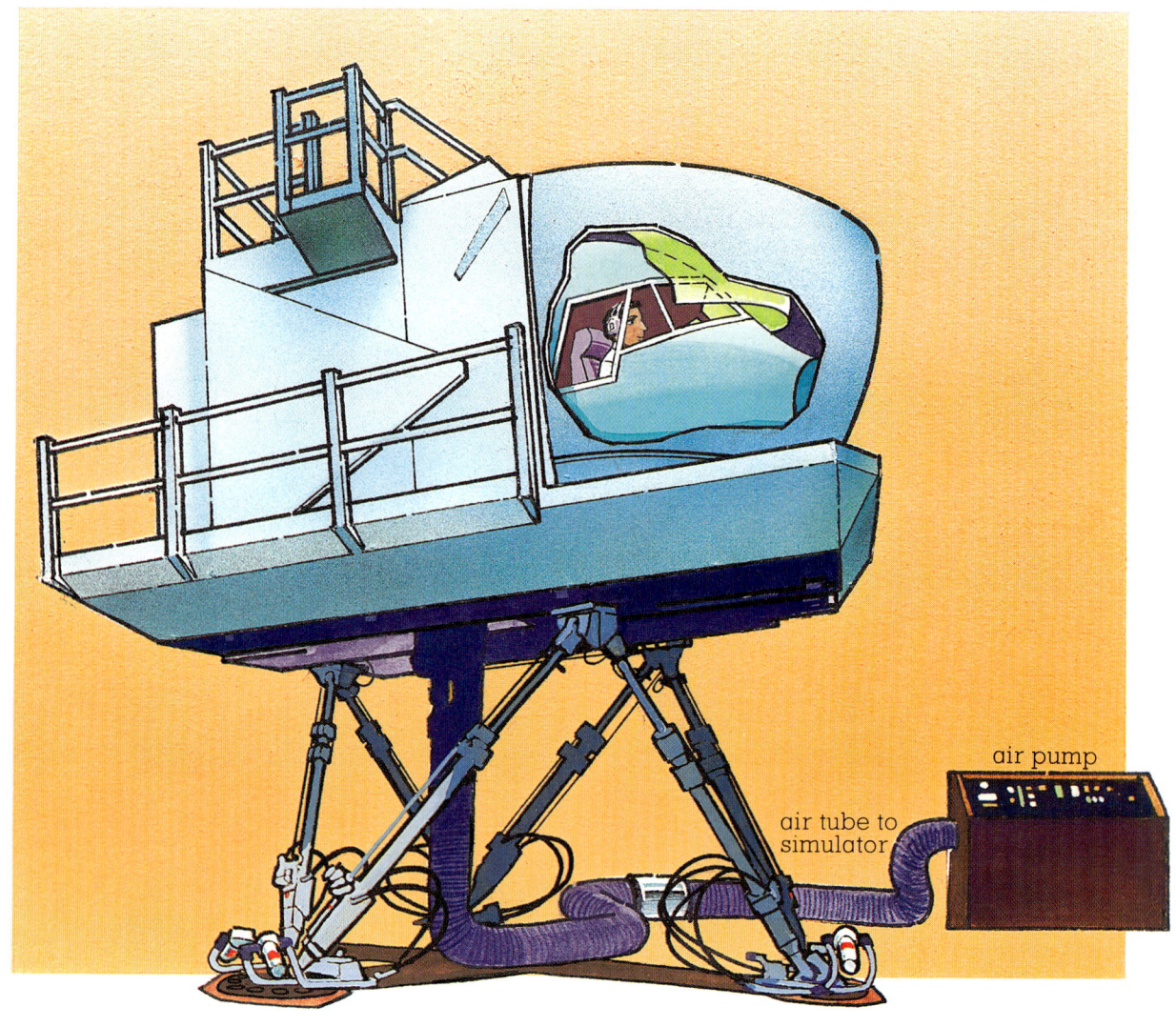

▲ This drawing shows the simulator 'cut-away' so that you can see the pilot inside

The simulator

This giant box on legs is called an aircraft simulator. Right in the middle of the box is a model of the pilot's cabin. The legs can move this cabin up and down and from side to side. They can tilt the cabin just as if it was in the air.

Everything in this model is exactly the same as in the real plane. The crew have special aircraft seats to sit in and all the controls work properly. There is no need for the crew to imagine anything.

Even the sounds and pictures are just like the real thing. Inside the cabin are lots of loudspeakers to make the noise of the aeroplane's engines, and outside the cabin window there is a special, very wide television picture.

The simulator is controlled by a large computer which is kept in the room next door.

The computer controls the motors which move the simulator's giant legs. It can make the sound effects and the television pictures. And it works very fast indeed.

The work of the computer

All computers, no matter what size, shape or colour they are, work by taking three steps. These are called *input, process* and *output*.

Every switch and lever and button in the simulator is connected to the computer by a cable underneath the floor.

If the pilot moves the controls in the simulator, a signal is sent down the cable to the computer. This signal is part of the *input* for the computer.

Then the computer has to work out what would happen if the pilot was flying a real plane. To do this, the computer needs a lot of information about how a real aeroplane would work. It needs to know how fast the engines can go, how much fuel they use up, what the engines would sound like and much, much more.

All this information is put into the computer before it can begin to work. It is stored on a magnetic disc, like the one in this photograph.

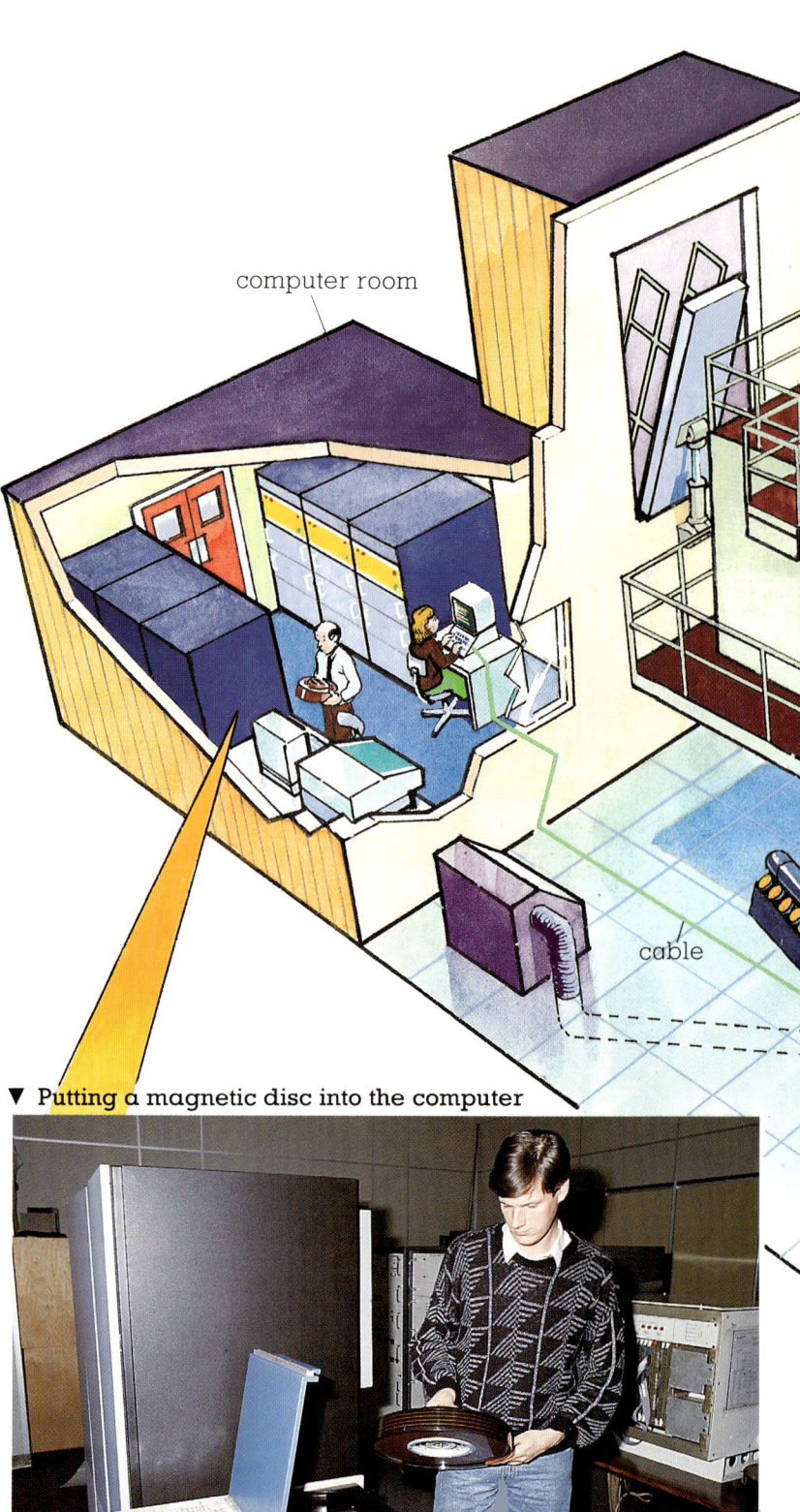

▼ **Putting a magnetic disc into the computer**

Inside the simulator. Each time the pilot moves the controls a message is sent to the computer along a cable under the floor

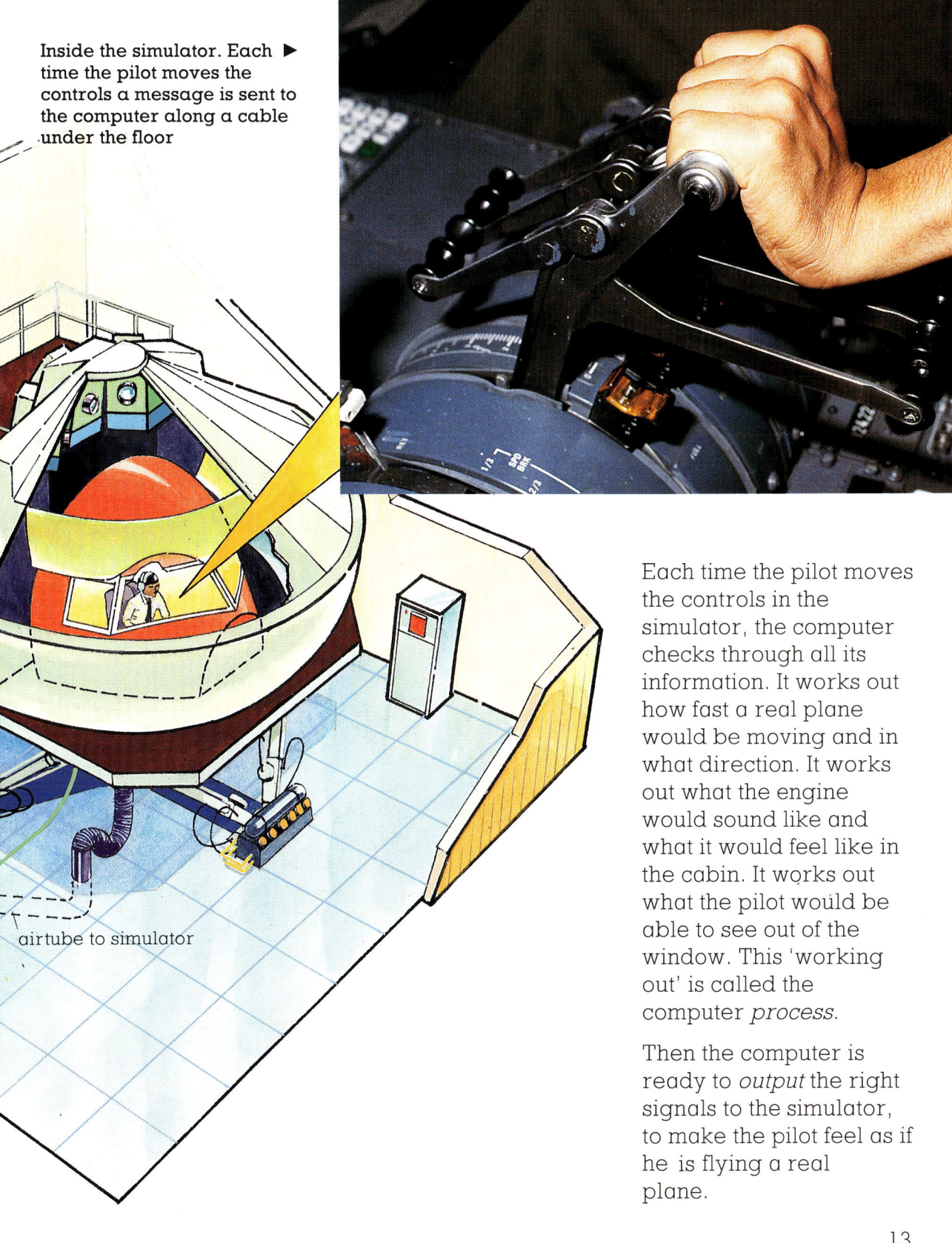

airtube to simulator

Each time the pilot moves the controls in the simulator, the computer checks through all its information. It works out how fast a real plane would be moving and in what direction. It works out what the engine would sound like and what it would feel like in the cabin. It works out what the pilot would be able to see out of the window. This 'working out' is called the computer *process*.

Then the computer is ready to *output* the right signals to the simulator, to make the pilot feel as if he is flying a real plane.

Sound and movement

The computer sends four different types of output to the simulator. It sends sound, movement and pictures. It also makes all the dials and instruments in the cabin show the right numbers and displays.

The sound comes through loudspeakers which are all round the pilot's cabin. The computer can make the sound of the engines going fast or slow. It can make an alarm to warn the pilot that something is wrong, or the sound of the 'bump' when the aeroplane lands on the runway.

The computer also controls the giant legs underneath the simulator. It can make the cabin go up or down, move from side to side and tilt forwards or backwards.

When a real plane takes off, the pilot and the passengers are pushed back into their seats by the movement.

The simulator doesn't take off, but it tips backwards a little bit and this pushes the pilot back into his seat. When the pilot looks through his window, he can't see that the cabin is tipping. He only sees a big picture of the runway getting further away.

Everything the pilot sees and hears and feels seems so real that he soon forgets he's in a simulator and feels just as if he's flying a real plane.

Simulating take-off ▶

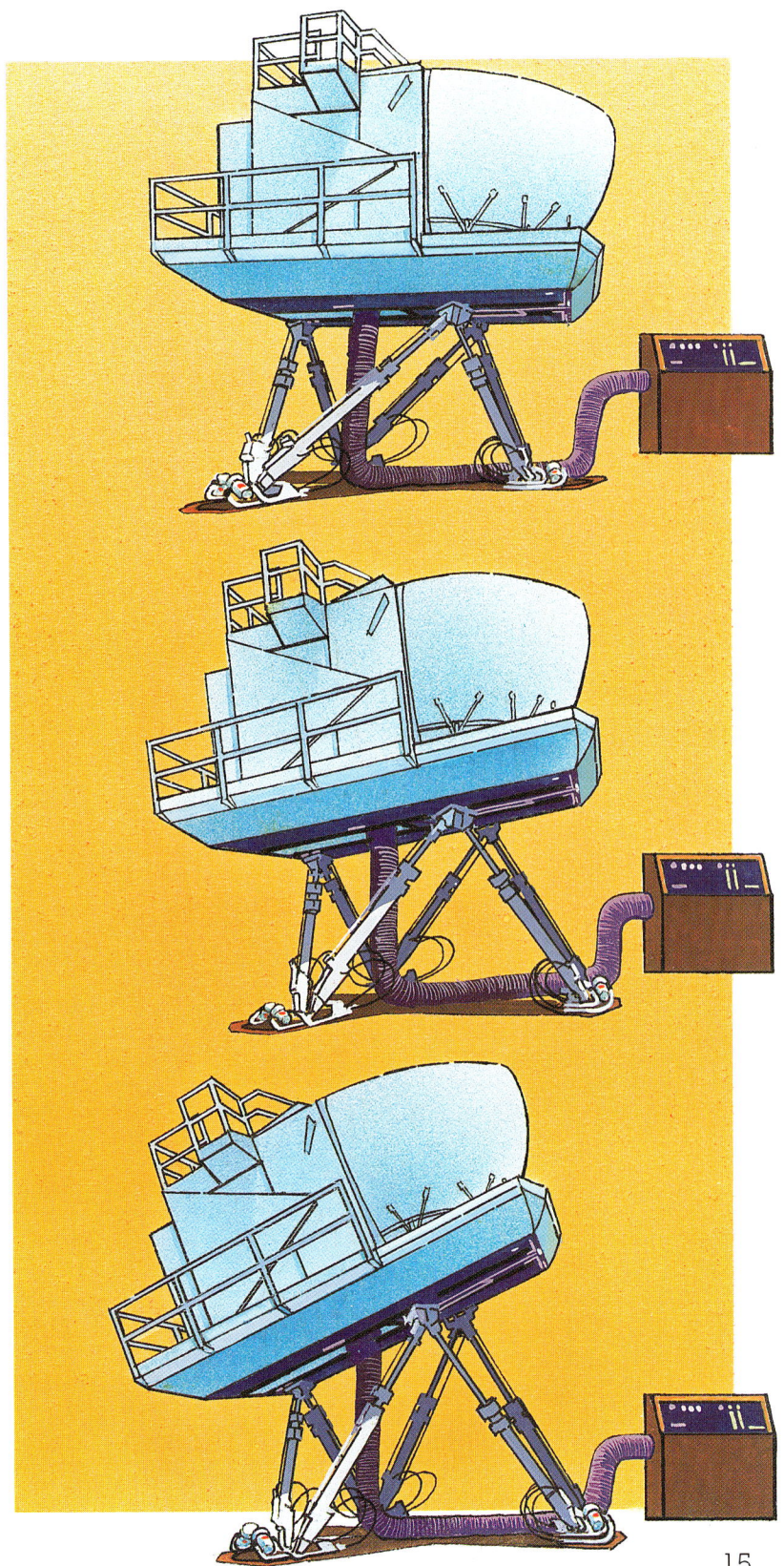

What the pilots sees

The computer makes sure that all the instruments in the cabin show the right numbers and positions. If the pilot moves the controls to make his plane go faster, the computer works out what would happen in a real plane.

The computer has to do some complicated calculations. It needs to be told where the pilot is pretending to fly to, how many passengers he has and what the weather is like. All these things will affect the speed of the plane. The computer can process all this information in a fraction of a second. Then it outputs the right signals to change the dial which shows the pilot's speed.

If the pilot moves the controls to go up or down, the dial which shows how high the plane is will also change.

The computer also makes sure that the right pictures come up outside the cabin window.

The pilot doesn't just see an ordinary television set outside the cabin window. It would be far too small and wouldn't look like the view from a real plane.

Outside the window of the cabin is a big curved screen. The pictures are projected on to this screen, rather like the pictures on a cinema screen. This means that the pilot can see the right view out of all the windows round the cabin.

Making the pictures

When the pilot first gets into the simulator, he tells the computer which airport he wants to fly from. If he chooses Hong Kong airport, a picture will come up outside the cabin windows showing exactly what he would see from a plane on the runway at Hong Kong.

Making the right pictures appear needs a lot of work by the computer. The computer doesn't have actual pictures of Hong Kong in its memory. But it does have a lot of information about the airport (and about other airports all over the world).

The computer knows the size of the airport. It knows where each runway, road and building is. It knows the position and colour of every single light around the airport. All this information is put into the computer before the simulator can be used.

The computer checks through all this information. It works out what the pilot would be able to see from the aeroplane. Then it outputs the signals to make the right picture.

The computer knows that if one building is behind another, the pilot would only be able to see the building in front.

When the pilot moves the controls to start the plane rolling down the runway, the computer makes the front building get bigger, as if the plane was getting nearer. When the pilot moves the controls for take off, the computer makes all the buildings look smaller.

Hundreds of times every second, the computer works out how far the pilot should have moved and what he would be able to see from his new position. It checks everything it knows about the airport in its memory and sends a new set of signals to make a different picture. It goes through this process and sends out new sets of signals more than a thousand times every minute.

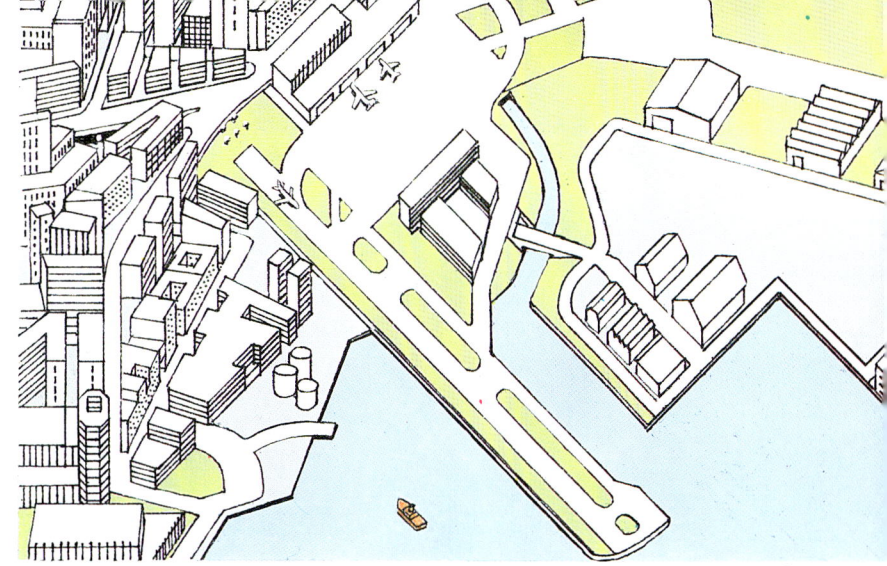
▲ The computer knows the size and position of the runway and the buildings

▲ The computer works out what the pilot would be able to see
▼ When the pilot moves the controls to make the plane take off, the computer changes the picture.

Flying in difficult conditions

This pilot and co-pilot are going to practise landing their plane.

First they can practise landing on a clear sunny day when they can easily see the runway. This is what they would see out of the cabin window.

Simulated runway on a sunny day ▶

Then the pilot's instructor can tell the computer to make it night time. The computer immediately changes the pictures to show what the airport looks like at night. It makes the runway lights very bright and the airport buildings difficult to see.

The crew can learn what it's like to land their plane in the middle of the night, although, outside the simulator, it is a sunny morning.

They can also ask the computer to show the runway in fog or rain or any other sort of terrible weather.

This is very useful because bad weather could be dangerous for a new pilot. The crew can get used to flying in all sorts of bad weather and if they make a mistake, there's no danger of anyone getting hurt.

▲ Simulated runway at night

▼ Simulated runway in fog

The pilot's instructor

There is one important difference between the cabin of a real plane and the cabin in the simulator. The simulator has an extra seat behind the pilot. It is for the instructor.

The instructor has his own computer terminal with a screen. This means that he can type instructions into the computer. The instructor can decide which kind of flight the pilot should practise. He can also make the computer pretend that something has gone wrong with the plane. Can you see all the terrible things which the instructor can choose from on his screen? He can make the computer pretend that the engines are overheating, or on fire.

In fact, planes are very safe and things don't go wrong very often. Still, we want the pilot to know what to do if something ever did go wrong.

The instructor can talk to the pilot through his microphone. He can pretend to be the man at the airport who tells the pilot when to bring the plane down. While the instructor is talking to the pilot, the computer can add in lots of crackles and hisses. This makes it sound as if a bad storm is interfering with the radio. It's good practice for the pilot.

On his computer screen, the instructor can see if the pilot is flying straight, or if he is too high or too low.

The computer keeps all this information in its memory. When the pilot comes out of the simulator he can have the information printed out to take away and read.

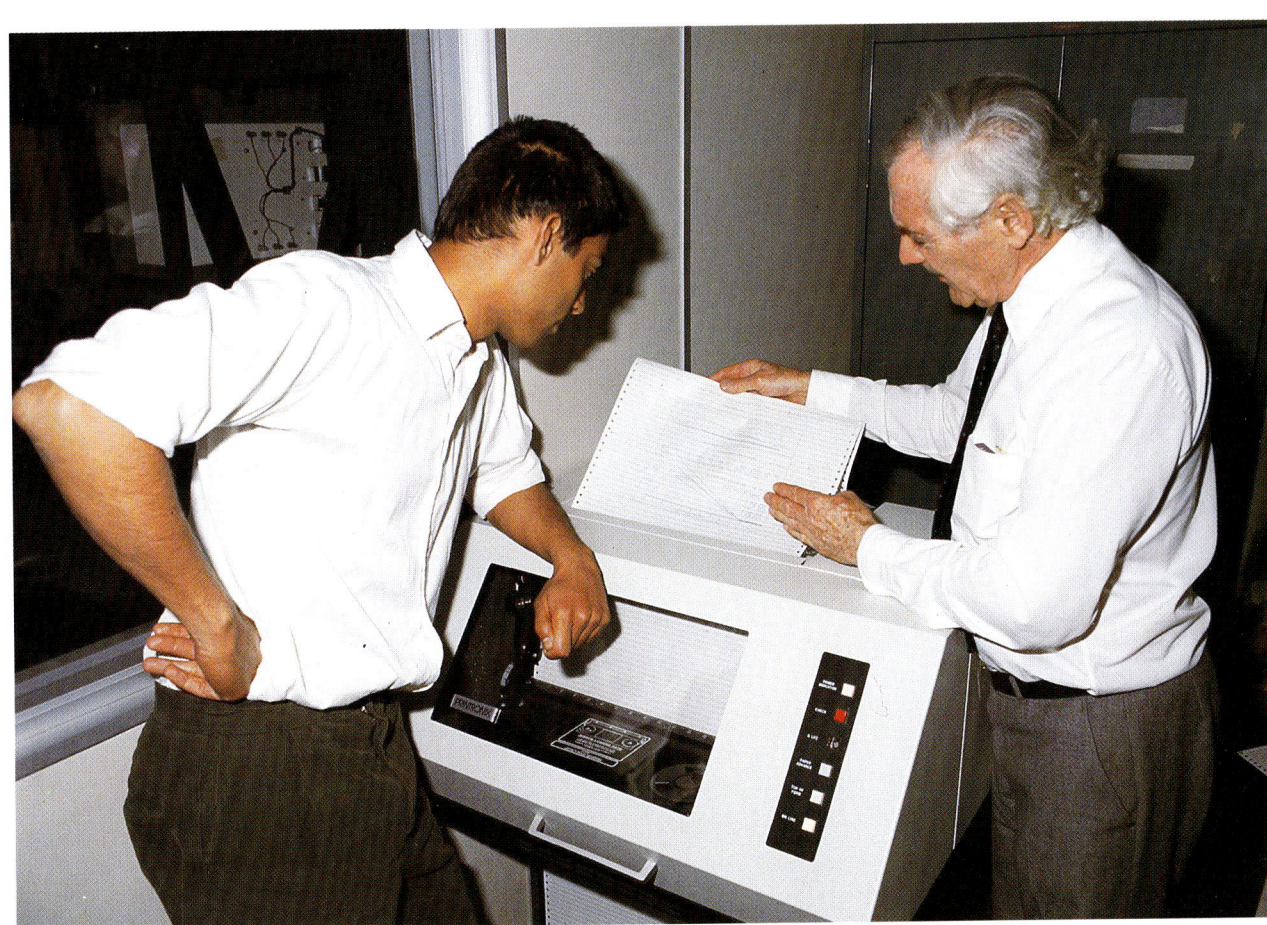

What else could simulators be used for?

The simulator lets the pilot practise flying a new plane. It's cheaper to use a simulator than it is to fly a real plane.

The pilot and his instructor can also practise things that would be too dangerous in a real plane.

The simulator lets pilots practise taking-off and landing at airports all over the world, without having to go there. As long as someone types in all the information about a new airport, the simulator can do the rest. A pilot can practise at three or four airports in a single morning.

The simulator is only useful because it seems real, and it seems real because it works so quickly.

As soon as the pilot moves a control, the simulator works out exactly what changes are needed to the sound, the picture and the movement.

The simulator can only work fast because it is controlled by a computer. Computers aren't clever, they just do what they are told. But they work very fast.

At the moment, simulators cost a lot of money to make. Usually only airlines and other very big companies can afford to buy them.

In the future, they will be cheaper. Can you think of any jobs that are difficult or dangerous to learn, where a simulator might be able to help, if it didn't cost too much?

If you learned to drive a car on a simulator, you could practise driving in the daytime and at night in one lesson.

You could practise driving in dry weather and in wet weather. You could practise on big motorways and on little roads.

What else can you think of? Perhaps you would like to ride on a bob-sleigh, or travel in a space-ship? Choose an adventure and imagine the sights, sounds and feelings that you would program into your computer.

Index

airport 18,19,21,23,24

cabin window 8,11,15,17,
 18,20
calculations 16
car 24
check-list 6,7
classroom 4
computer 2,8,11,12,13,14,
 15,16,17,18,19,21,22,23,24
computer screen 22,23
computer terminal 22
controls 4,5,6,8,9,10,12,13,
 16,19,24
co-pilot 4,5,6,20
crash 7
crew 5,7,10,21

day-time 20,24
dials 4,14,16
difficult conditions 20,21

emergency 7
engineer 4,5,6,7
engines 6,9,11,12,13,14,22

fire 7,22
'flying machine' 9,10
fog 21
fuel 6,12

information 12,13,16,18,19,
 23,24
input 12
instructor 6,21,22,23,24

landing 6,20,21,23,24
legs 10,11,15
loudspeakers 10,14

magnetic disc 12
memory 18,19,23
microphone 23
mistakes 3,7,21
model cabin
 in classroom 4,5,6,7,10
 in simulator 11,14,15,
  16,17,22
movement 10,11,14,15,24

night-time 21,24

output 12,13,14,16,19

passengers 15,16
pictures 8,9,11,14,15,17,
 18,19,21,24
print-out 23
process 12,13,16,19
projector 17

radio 23
rain 21
runway 14,15,18,19,20,21

screen 17
seats 4,5,10,15,22
signal 12,13,16,19
simulator 10,11,12,13,
 14,15,18,21,22,23,24
speed 16

take-off 6,15,24

view 8,17

weather 16,21,24

25